Text copyright © 1984, 2015 by Harriet Ziefert
Illustrations copyright © 2015 by Fred Blunt
All rights reserved
CIP data is available.
Published in the United States 2015 by
🍎 Blue Apple Books
515 Valley Street, Maplewood, NJ 07040
www.blueapplebooks.com

Printed in China
Paperback ISBN: 978-1-60905-461-8
Hardcover ISBN: 978-1-60905-577-6

1 3 5 7 9 10 8 6 4 2
02/15

The BANANA BUNCH
and the
Magic Show

by Harriet Ziefert

illustrations by Fred Blunt

BLUE APPLE

Meet
The BANANA BUNCH

Lucas

Molly

Scruffy

Jack

Sue

Sam

Scott

Chapter One
The Picnic

Here's a group of friends.

They call themselves the Banana Bunch.

Right now, they're off to a picnic!

You can go with them.

Come on and meet the gang.

There's Lucas, Sam, Jack,

Molly, Sue, Scott, and Scruffy.

Lucas wears glasses. Sam has freckles.

Jack is tall, and Molly is not.

Sue has braids, and Scott does not.

And Scruffy is Scruffy. (He's also Molly's dog.)

They have boxes and bags, balls and bats—

and a blanket, too!

They're looking for a good spot for their stuff.

Sam shouts, "I think I found a great place.

The ground is flat. We can spread the

blanket and take off our socks and shoes."

Everyone agrees.

Jack and Molly spread the blanket.

Scruffy sits in the middle while Sam puts heavy

rocks on the corners.

"Let's eat our sandwiches now," says Jack.

"But we just got here," says Lucas.

"If you're not hungry, you can wait,"

answers Jack.

"But I'm eating now!"

"Me, too!" says Sam.

"Me, too!" says Sue.

"Me, too!" says Molly.

"*Arf! Arf!*" says Scruffy.

Everybody starts to eat.

"Oops! I dropped my jelly sandwich!"

cries Molly.

"Call Scruffy," someone says. "He's good at

cleaning up messes."

SCRUFFY! SCRUFFY!

CAN YOU CLEAN THIS, SCRUFFY?

"Look," says Sue, "an inchworm is walking up my arm."

"And a mosquito is drinking from my foot!" cries Scott. "OUCH!"

"I think we'd better clean up before the ants arrive!" says Lucas.

The kids mumble "okay" and crumple up their papers.

Molly and Scott find a basket for garbage.

"What should we do now?" asks Jack.

"I have an idea," says Lucas.

"Let's play a game of hide-and-seek."

"I'll be 'IT,'" says Molly.

"Hurry up and let's start."

Molly heads toward a big tree.

Everybody else thinks of a direction to run

in after Molly begins to count.

When Molly gets to the tree, she closes her eyes.

"NO PEEKING!" shouts Sam.

"NO CHEATING!" yells Sue.

"COUNT TO FIFTY," says Lucas.

"AND COUNT SLOWLY!" says Sam.

"I'm ready!" shouts Molly.

She counts:

"1, 2, 3, 4, 5, 6, 7, 8, 9 . . . "

By now, almost everyone is out of sight.

Molly keeps on counting:

"10, 11, 12, 13, 14, 15 . . ."

There are a few bushes moving, but that's all.

Molly is almost done:

". . . 35, 36, 37, 38, 39, 40, 41, 42, 43, 44, 45, 46, 47, 48, 49 . . .

50! ANYONE AROUND MY BASE IS IT!"

When Molly opens her eyes, it seems as if she is all alone in the park.

Chapter Two

Smart Dog

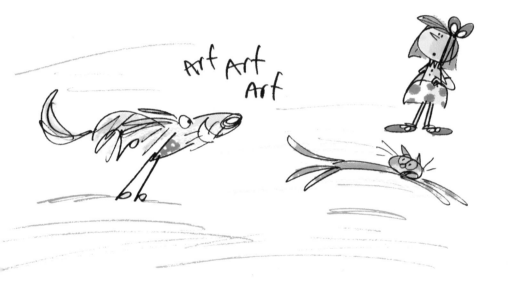

Molly runs in the direction of the duck pond.

But she doesn't find anybody—except Scruffy.

And he is chasing a cat.

When the cat runs up a tree, Scruffy runs
after Molly.

Molly doesn't mind Scruffy tagging along.

Molly looks and looks, but she can't
find anybody.

She's upset.

She bends down and whispers something
to Scruffy.

Scruffy is off!

He runs to some bushes.

He sniffs.

He finds Lucas and Sam!

Then Scruffy runs to a park bench.

He sniffs some more.

He finds Sue.

When he stands in front of a statue and
barks, the rest of the gang comes out.

"You cheated!" everyone shouts at Molly.

"This game is not fair!" Jack yells.

Molly answers, "Scruffy's my dog, and
I played fair!"

"You can't play fair with a dog around,"
says Sue.

"So let's play something else."

"Okay," says Jack. "Does everyone remember
how to play Spud?"

"Sure we do," says Lucas, "we're not dumb!"

"So let's get started," says Jack.

"I'll give each of you a number.
And keep your number a secret!"

Sue gets the ball.

She throws it in the air and shouts:

"FIVE!"

Everyone runs—except Lucas.

Lucas's number is also five, and he has to catch the ball.

When he gets it, he yells "SPUD!"

Everyone stops when they hear "SPUD!"

Lucas takes three steps and tries

to hit Sam with the ball.

Lucas throws and misses!

So Lucas has "S."

Now Lucas throws the ball in the air

and shouts: "THREE!"

That is Scott's number.

Scott runs for the ball.

But so does Scruffy.

Who gets the ball?

Of course—it's Scruffy!

Scruffy will not give the ball to Scott.

Scott says, "Molly, come here and talk
to this dog!"

Molly whispers into Scruffy's ear.

Scruffy listens, then he smiles and runs away.

Scruffy always seems to understand just what Molly is saying.

Chapter Three

The Password

"I'm tired!' says Lucas.

"Me, too!" says Sue.

"What a day!" says Sam. "Let's head back
   to the clubhouse."

Lucas, Sam, Jack,

Molly, Sue and Scott all walk together.

Jack, who always seems to think about

food, shouts: "Look, there's the ice cream man!

Let's get some before the truck drives away."

"What'll it be, kids?" asks the ice cream man.

"I want a double chocolate fudge pop,"

says Molly.

"So do I," says Lucas.

"I want an orange bar," says Scott,

licking his lips.

"We want vanilla cones," say Sue and Sam.

"And I'll have an ice cream sandwich,"

says Jack.

Everyone in the club loves ice cream.

What's your favorite kind?

They finish their ice cream quickly.

Then they walk slowly toward their clubhouse.

When they get there, Jack shouts,

"Scruffy BEAT US HOME!"

"Scruffy did exactly what I told him to do,"
says Molly.

"I sent him to the clubhouse so he
wouldn't bother us anymore."

"Can we have a meeting?" asks Sue.

"If it's short!" grumbles Lucas.

37

The meeting comes to order. Sam says,
"I've been thinking. This club is
missing something.
We're missing something important!"

Everyone wonders what's missing.

The club has members.

The club has membership cards.

The club has a clubhouse.

What else does it need?

"We need a password," says Sam.

"Who has an idea?"

Everyone is quiet.

"Whoever has an idea, speak up!" says Sue.

But no one says anything.

Finally, Jack stands up.

He says, "I think I know a good word."

Jack doesn't want to say the word out loud,

so he walks around and whispers it into each

person's ear.

Lucas, Sam, Molly,

Sue, Scott, and Scruffy like the word a lot.

They promise to keep it a secret.

(Since you can keep a secret, Scruffy will

tell you the password…)

Chapter Four
A Money-Making Idea

"This club needs to earn money," says Sue.

"So how can we raise some?" asks Sam.

At first, no one answers.

"We can sell lemonade," says Lucas.

"Too boring!" answers Molly.

"We can have a car wash," says Sue.

"Too wet!" says Scott.

"Doesn't anybody have a really good idea?"
Lucas complains.

"I do!" says Jack. "I have the best idea."

"Well, what's your great idea?" Lucas asks.

Jack answers, "My idea is a magic show.
We can build a stage right in front of
our clubhouse."

"Wish you lots of luck," mumbles Lucas.

"Do you really think we can do it?" asks Sam.

"Sure we can," says Jack.

"How much can we charge?" Scott asks.

"Fifty cents!" says Molly. "We need the money!"

"Well, for fifty cents," says Sam, "each one of us
had better learn a really good trick!"

"Arf! Arf!" says Scruffy, agreeing with Sam.

Jack says, "I think we should vote
about the magic show.
Yeses stand up and nos stay down."

Everyone stands up except Lucas.

There are five yeses and one no,
plus one bow-wow.

So Jack says, "Okay, we'll have the show!"

"The meeting is over now," says Molly. "It's almost dinnertime, and Scruffy wants to go home."

Sue says, "Let's meet tomorrow right after breakfast. Tonight, think about magic tricks!"

Chapter Five

Getting Ready

They start early the next day.

They need a stage, a table, old sheets, wooden

boards, and all kinds of props.

Luckily, someone has a magic wand.

There is a lot to do, but they work hard.

"I learned two card tricks," says Lucas.

"I couldn't learn any!" complains Jack.

"Will you teach me one?"

"Sure," says Lucas. "Pick a card."

Lucas tells him to put the card in the middle
of the deck.

Then Lucas says, "I'm going to tell you the
secret of this trick. I peek at the bottom card
in the deck before I start."

"Does every trick have a secret?" asks Jack.

"Sure," says Molly, "even the mind-reading
   trick that I learned has one!"

"Then, to be a great magician, I just have to
   learn a secret!" says Jack.

"We're going to perform the most spectacular
trick," say Sue and Scott.

"We're going to make Scruffy vanish into thin air!"

"That's impossible!" says Molly.

"How will you do it?" asks Jack.

"That's our secret," says Scott.

"Well," says Molly, "whatever you do,
you'd better not lose my dog."

A few days later, the work is almost done.

Lucas and Jack build a stage.

They use old sheets and boards.

"Watch where you step!" yells Lucas as

Sue tries to walk across the stage.

Sam sets up chairs.

Sue finishes the disappearing box.

Scott digs, and Scruffy helps.

They seem to be making a big hole—

or maybe a tunnel?

Scott won't say what they are doing.

He just says it's important for their trick.

Lucas has posters.

Jack tries to hang them up.

"Be careful or you'll bang that nail right
into my finger!" shouts Lucas.

Everyone sells tickets.

Lots of kids on the block are interested in magic, so tickets sell pretty fast.

Finally, everything is ready.

"I'm so nervous," says Sam.

"I'll do my trick first," says Molly.

"We'll save ours for last," says Sue.

Chapter Six

Scruffy Steals the Show

At 2 p.m., kids start arriving.

Sam collects tickets.

Everyone takes their seats.

Sue walks onto the stage.

"Quiet," she says, "the show is about to begin.

I now present MOLLY THE MIND READER."

Molly walks on stage.

She closes her eyes and begins.

"My trick requires great concentration,

so please be very quiet."

Molly slowly opens her eyes.

She asks a person from the audience

to write a number between one and ten

on a piece of paper.

Billy Maguire writes a number.

When Billy hands the paper to Molly,

she puts it behind her back.

Everyone is quiet.

Suddenly, Molly says, "I've got it!

Your number is seven!"

"You're right!" says Billy. "How did you know?

Molly does not tell her secret.

She bows as the audience claps.

Lucas and Jack do their card tricks.

They are great.

Almost everybody is fooled.

Then Sam does the disappearing coin trick.

Everybody claps.

This is a real magic show!

When Sam finishes his trick, he waits

for everyone's attention.

Then he speaks: "Ladies and gentlemen,

for the most spectacular part of the show,

I now present SUE AND SCOTT AND THE

VANISHING DOG!"

Sue puts the disappearing box on stage.

Scott and Scruffy follow.

Scott speaks: "Here we have an ordinary wooden box."

Sue says, "Scruffy, get into the box. Silence in the audience, please."

Scruffy climbs into the box.

Scott makes sure it is tightly closed.

Now for the magic wand and the magic words:
"PUDS! DUBS! SPUDS!"

Scott waves the wand, and Sue claps

her hands twice. *Clap! Clap!*

Then Sue tells Scott to open the box.

Everyone in the audience is surprised.

"He's really gone!" shouts a boy.

"Vanished!" says a girl.

"How did you do it?" calls another.

Sue smiles but doesn't answer.

Scott steps forward and says,

"Since you're all wondering how we did

our last trick, just listen to what

Scruffy is saying.

He's explaining our secret!"

Then everyone in the gang comes on stage.

They all bow, and someone says,

"COME BACK AGAIN SOON FOR MORE
FUN WITH THE BANANA BUNCH."

Activities

- Learn a magic trick, then be a "magician."

- Teach a magic trick to a friend.

- Make a list of what Scruffy does that a real dog could not. Your list should include at least six different behaviors.